Better Day Coming

A Dream, A Journey, A New Beginning

Rose Maiolo Armen
Illustrated by Valeria Leonova

❧ ❧ ❧

Embark on my father's immigration story from Nardodipace, Italy to the United States in 1951. This story is depicted by a mouse sharing his dream to leave his hometown in Italy for a better life in a peculiar new country.

Join Topolino Garibaldi as he grows from a youngster exploring the hills of Calabria to a mature and responsible Italian immigrant living in the hope filled land of America.

Acknowledgement to Blueberry

Dedication

❧⟡ ⟡❧

To my father
Garibaldi Maiolo
The BEST daddy a girl could ever have.

My father immigrated from Nardodipace, Italy to the United States in 1951. This would be the first of many trips that he made to this side of the Atlantic Ocean.
My family is so proud of our father's strength, courage, and determination to forge out a new life in a strange country. We will be forever grateful for his many sacrifices to build a new life for his family in an unfamiliar land.

Better Day Coming
A recurring sentiment my father would express to renew his hope for brighter and happier days ahead.
My father's legacy has revealed to me the keys to a peaceful and fulfilling life...

Dream Big-Work Hard-Be Grateful
As you travel with Topolino Garibaldi on his wondrous and sometimes arduous journey, look carefully to find a key in the illustrations. The key is a symbol of faith. With faith, my father was able to achieve his dreams.

Topolino Garibaldi, a very special little mouse, was born in a faraway country, called Italy. His petite hometown named *Nardodipace* is a hidden gem in the mountainous hills of southern Calabria. Nardodipace was settled in the 1800's and its name means a "City of Peace". How appropriate for this village populated by a few peaceful and kindhearted families.

Back in the day, Nardodipace was a teeny, tiny village brimming with hardworking families, all living close together, and helping each other in the good times, and especially in the challenging times. The town had one small church centered in the middle and one priest who walked to the neighboring towns to offer comfort and counsel to the neighbors.

All the busy neighbors had to grow their own food and take care of their animals. These skillful townspeople made their own cheese, pasta, bread, olive oil and something else that was important for daily living... *sapone* or soap!

Yes, our friend Topolino Garibaldi
consumed several hours of his day
making soap, with his Mamma Rosaria.

A big iron pot was put into action to cook
animal fat, or sometimes just plain olive
oil, mixed with water over a red hot fire.

It was Mamma and her son's
responsibility to continuously stir the hot
pot with a giraffe neck wooden spoon
until the fat had all melted in the scalding
hot water.

Once that was completed, the liquid had
to cool down before it was poured into
trays to harden. A special razor sharp
knife was used to cut up chunks of soap
to be used and sold by Topolino's family.

Everyone living in Nardodipace had a job,
even the pets!

Rosa the mule was Topolino's family pet,
and she helped with the family business for
sixteen long years.

It was Topolino's job to pack up the goods
to be traded or sold and load them into
Rosa's saddlebags.

Together they traveled to nearby towns to
deliver the goods and return back home
with new supplies.

The little mouse always loaded his pockets
with a few rock hard chestnuts and some
dry, stale bread to snack on along
the wooded paths.

Sometimes Rosa and Topolino
walked for days and nights,
to reach their destination.

You see, it was his job to help the family
earn money by selling everything that Rosa
was carrying, and sometimes that may have
taken a few long days to accomplish.

Growing up in this small, hillside village of Nardodipace proved to be difficult. Homes did not have electricity, running water, or toilets. Imagine bathing in a water hole at the edge of the village, or washing your clothes in a cold river using stones to rub out the dirty stains. Life was busy, and most chores had to be done by hand.

Everyone, young and old, had to pitch in and provide for their family's survival. The young children were expected to walk to nearby towns to attend school in one room classrooms, after rising early to do their chores.

Children often decided on their own when to go to school, and when to stay back and finish their chores. Attendance wasn't very important, and sometimes it was considered noble to skip school and help your family instead.

So busy little Topolino Garibaldi stopped going to school by the age of eight. He had to take on the family business of importing and exporting supplies around the small villages of southern Calabria.

Life was hard for the family and Topolino Garibaldi had some far fetched fantasies of running away in search of new and awesome adventures!

He had dreams and visions of wanting to see what life would be like on the other side of the world called AMERICA! After all, his father Domenico had made that incredible trip to the other side... eighteen times!

Wishful thinking and encouragement from his family helped him realize that it was time for the young *paisano* to seek out new experiences in this peculiar and unfamiliar country named America. Topolino Garibaldi was about to go on the journey of his life, encountering many new and strange surroundings.

He kept wondering and asking himself, *"How am I going to be brave enough to make my dreams come true?"*

One chilly autumn morning in 1951,
the young nineteen year old
decided it was the perfect time
to set sail on his
boundless transatlantic excursion.

Naturally Topolino Garibaldi
was a little bit sad and weepy
to leave his family and hometown
but
he said his goodbyes, traveled to Naples
and then hopped
on a big ship
named the *Fiorello LaGuardia*.

On this enormous boat he was terribly hungry, lonely, and extremely seasick. Every so often he scurried around looking for food scraps and places to sleep away from the other passengers. After twenty-one days of being tossed around on the vessel, he woke up. He realized that the ship had stopped moving, and the passengers were a lot noisier than they had ever been before. *Why all of these changes and why had the water stopped moving the ship?*

It was Thursday, December 13, 1951, and on this cold and frosty morning the mammoth ship had finally arrived in New York City.

Thunderous cheers frightened Topolino Garibaldi, as he watched the passengers hugging, and crying happy tears as they all stepped off the gangplank onto a new land, alive with scores of opportunities to be sniffed out.

Topolino was painfully shy. He had to be extremely cautious exiting the ship so that no one would stop and try to talk to him. He carefully darted around all the others and managed to run out and step onto the bustling streets of New York City.

While roaming the surrounding
neighborhoods
his first thought was to seek out
some dry, warm clothes,
delicious food,
and a safe place
to bunk for the night.

The overflowing streets were
congested, deafening,
and
very frightening,
for an inexperienced Italian mouse,
but
he tried be brave and solve his problems.

Despite all his worries, the tired little mouse found an old brick building. He decided to slip into a hole used as a coal chute. He hoped it might lead to a warm place.

Topolino briskly forced his way in through the hole and fell into a dark space. He was terrified, but he slowly climbed out of the dark space, looked around, and realized he had fallen into a pile of midnight black colored coal!

Immediately feeling safe, he ventured over to the cast iron, coal burning stove to warm up his nose and toes. He loved the familiar sight and started scurrying around and tripping over lots of boots and shoes.

It was after he made another connection with the distinctive scent of leather that he realized he was inside a cobbler's shop. Feeling comfortable inside the warm cozy shop, Topolino decided to snuggle down for the long night.

His tummy kept growling as he scooted around the shoe repair shop looking for a tasty morsel. Sadly he didn't find any crumbs, so he was forced to venture back outside to seek out some food.

As he ran around the streets, he stopped because he smelled some familiar smells again, just like the smells he remembered from Nardodipace. As he rushed ahead, the smells became overpowering and his tummy growled and roared with hunger.

Topolino stopped short and ran through an open doorway. Once inside the building he looked around and read the sign, *La Cucina di Mafalda, a fine Italian dining experience.*

Well, the little mouse found oodles of long stringy noodles covered in dark red tomato sauce, with tender soft shavings of Parmesan cheese mixed in, and a hunk of brown crusty bread to fill his belly. His first feast in America was a fine Italian meal fit for a little Italian mouse stepping foot right off the boat!

The sun was beginning to set on the very frosty day, so the shivering and worried little mouse had to remember his path back home to the shoe repair shop.

After running through unending streets, dodging sidewalk walkers, and cars, he finally arrived back home.

He was very winded, but proud he had found his way back home before the beautiful pinkish orange sunset would begin to turn into a spooky black night.

He climbed in again, through the coal chute, and smiled when he looked around at his new home. Running around the shop, he decided that he would make his bed in the attic where he could peek out at the stars through the wide slits in the roof.

Topolino Garibaldi was becoming homesick, but gazing up at the stars made him feel close to his family.

Upon resting his weary head on the pillow he would envision his Mamma, Papà, *fratello* Bruno, and his beloved Nardodipace.

All of his memories of being back home in Italy helped to comfort him, so that he could fall into a deep restful sleep.

Topolino enjoyed living in his new safe home, but one thing really annoyed him. The shop owner was messy and disorganized!

The shop looked like a whirlwind had blown through causing a jumbled pile of stuff to be scattered everywhere.

The floor was littered with shoes, boots, boxes, leather pieces, thread spools, needles of all sizes, tools, and more tools covering every inch in this small shop!

One night after returning from another visit to
La Cucina di Mafalda, the little mouse decided that it
was time to straighten out this shameful looking shop.
After all, now it was his house too!

First, he organized the shoes, and boots, and that was
no easy task for an inexperienced mouse. The tools were
gathered and shelved and the floors swept before he
decided he should call it a day and go to bed.

As he started to run up to his bedroom in the attic, he
turned and smiled as he looked around at the tidy shop.

Well, you can imagine how excited Rocco, the storekeeper, was when he stepped into his perfect looking shop the next morning.

Rocco was puzzled but relieved that he didn't have to deal with his messy workshop on this chilly winter morning.

For the next few weeks, the cleanup helper returned every night to tidy up the shop. Rocco would smile and be amazed at how lovely the shop looked, but deep down he continued to be puzzled as to who would be doing this nice thing for him.

No one else had the keys to the shop, so of course the only explanation was that there was some kind of after dark magic happening in the shop, but what was it all about?

Day after day, Topolino waited until the shop closed and then he went about his business of cleaning which made him feel proud and useful.

Still though, he had a dull ache in his heart from missing his family and wanting so badly to make a new friend.

He would spend his days peeking out at Rocco while he was repairing shoes and talking to his beloved customers, and sadly, the poor little mouse didn't have a friend to talk to.

One night Topolino Garibaldi decided he needed a friend, so he scratched out an invitation to Rocco inviting him to stay for dinner at the shop tomorrow night.

He wrote: *Mio caro amico Rocco, I have enjoyed cleaning your shop and I think we should meet each other. Le prego di venire qui per la cena stasera alle otto. Tu amico, Garibaldi*

After writing the invitation, Topolino ventured out to find
some pasta, bread, cheese, and olives
at his favorite neighborhood restaurant,
La Cucina di Mafalda,
to prepare for a meal with his new friend Rocco.

At 8:00 the next morning, Rocco was surprised to see the
invitation placed on his work bench.

The excitement showed in Rocco's big grin, and he felt butterflies in his tummy to finally be able to meet his new friend. Rocco worked all day, but decided to close the shop a bit earlier so that he could wash up and get ready for *cena* with his new *amico*.

As soon as the shop was closed, Topolino swept the floor and set up a delicious dinner on the cobbler's workbench. He was sprinting around and trying to make the shop look fabulous, when suddenly he heard footsteps coming. Topolino skedaddled out the back door to hide.

The magical time had arrived for the two friends to greet each other. Rocco unlocked the door, and cautiously walked into the dimly lit room.

He quickly glanced around at his surroundings. Of course, he didn't see anyone there, but he smiled when he caught sight of the cobbler's workbench. In a very nervous voice, he timidly called out, "*Buonasera, sono arrivato per la cena*".

Quietly in the corner of the room.
Topolino Garibaldi poked his head
into the room from the back door.
All decked out in a new blue jacket, and
feeling rather handsome, he greeted the
shop owner by bellowing out,
"Buonasera Rocco!"

Startled at first, but then feeling
comfortable, Rocco stepped over to the
workbench to sit down as his little friend
started scooping out some of the
Italian delicacies.

An evening of sharing stories about
New York and Nardodipace went late
into the night.

It was a lovely evening shared by
two new friends,
who would become
two forever friends.

Rocco promised Topolino that he would
help him make America
his new home with many new but
challenging opportunities.

As Rocco locked up his shop for the night,
Topolino scooted upstairs,
jumped into his cozy bed,
and fluffed up his pillow.

He thought a lot about his future and for
the first time he knew what he wanted.
He quickly fell into a deep sleep as he kept
hearing
the melodious words....

"Welcome to America, Topolino Garibaldi.
I will help you make a new life here.
You will work hard but be brave
and courageous!"

It will be a good life!"

Where will Topolino's journey take him?
Do you think Topolino should stay in America
and make a new life? Did you find all the keys?

Translation

Buonasera, sono arrivato per la cena
- Good evening, I have arrived for dinner

Fratello - Brother
La Cucina di Mafalda - Mafalda's Kitchen

**"Le prego di venire qui per la
cena stasera alle otto."
Tu amico, Garibaldi**
- Please come here for dinner tonight at 8:00.
Your friend, Garibaldi

Mio caro amico - My dear friend
Nardodipace - Nar-do-di-pa-ce,
a tiny town in Calabria
Paisano - Male Peasant Friend
Sapone - Soap
Topolino - Little Mouse